STO

FRIEND
OF ACPL

DO NOT REMOVE
CARDS FROM POCKET

4\93

ALVIN'S
Famous No-Horse

*Here are some other
Redfeather Books from Henry Holt*

William Harry Harding

ALVIN'S Famous No-Horse

Illustrated by Michael Chesworth

A REDFEATHER BOOK
Henry Holt and Company • New York

Text copyright © 1992 by William Harry Harding
Illustrations copyright © 1992 by Michael Chesworth
All rights reserved, including the right to reproduce
this book or portions thereof in any form.
First edition
Published by Henry Holt and Company, Inc.,
115 West 18th Street, New York, New York 10011.
Published simultaneously in Canada by Fitzhenry & Whiteside Ltd.,
91 Granton Drive, Richmond Hill, Ontario L4B 2N5.

Library of Congress Cataloging-in-Publication Data
Harding, William Harry.
Alvin's famous no-horse / William Harry Harding:
illustrated by Michael Chesworth.
(A Redfeather book)
Summary: With encouragement from his teacher and help
from his classmates, eight-year-old Alvin struggles with his
efforts to draw a horse for the third-grade art exhibit.
ISBN 0-8050-2227-9
[1. Drawing—Fiction.   2. Artists—Fiction.   3. Schools—Fiction.]
I. Chesworth, Michael, ill.   II. Title.   III. Series.
PZ7.H2183A1   1992
[Fic]—dc20   92-13834

Printed in the United States of America
on acid-free paper. ∞
1   3   5   7   9   10   8   6   4   2

In memory of my own Mrs. Casey
and for Rachel Rose   —W. H. H.

To Beth   —M. C.

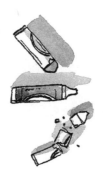

ALVIN'S
Famous No-Horse

Mrs. Casey wasn't wearing her test face. Maybe she had forgotten about her Every Monday Spelling Quiz. Alvin hoped so. He still had trouble with *accommodate*. That word didn't look right no matter how many *c*'s or *m*'s he tried it with. Mrs. C was sure to put it on the test.

She was sitting on the edge of her desk, squinting at the wall as if trying to read one of the hand-printed posters back there—probably her favorite, DOS and DON'TS. Everybody said that poster had been up there since the Live Oak Valley School opened, back when Mrs. Casey was the principal too and not just the third-grade teacher.

She blinked—even her eyelashes were silver—and her hands went together fast, but those bony fingers didn't make a sound. "I've never had a class so proficient in spelling," Mrs. Casey said, smiling when she came to *proficient*, a word on this week's list. Every other third grade probably got easy words, like *saddle* and *ranch*. Alvin and his class got the Mrs. C words.

"So instead of going on to more difficult words," Mrs. Casey said, walking to the cabinet near the bookcases, "we'll spend our spelling time on something new. Art—as a reward for both of us." The metal door creaked open. She dug into a box and came out with a handful of colored markers. "You know, I once thought of being an artist."

No matter how hard he looked at her, Alvin couldn't picture Mrs. C drawing or painting anything. He couldn't imagine her spilling paint on her green dress, either.

Moving up and down the rows of desks, she passed out the markers. Alvin got a brown one with a fat tip. Loretta, who sat right in front of him, near enough to touch Mrs. Casey's dark wood desk, got a red marker. Great, Alvin thought. Now I'll have to swim through drawings of red cats just to go eat lunch.

Loretta was a good runner, faster than some boys—not Roy, of course, because nobody in Live Oak except Jesse was as fast as Roy, and Jesse was in high school

and on the track team there—but when it came to drawing or painting or doing arts and crafts, all Loretta ever made were her dumb cats. She even had dresses with cats on them.

"We'll have an art exhibit." Mrs. Casey picked up a piece of chalk and printed EXHIBIT on the blackboard. "For Parents' Night on Friday. Much more interesting than merely putting up the words you've learned to spell." She peered over the top of her small square glasses. "Although we will still be doing that, too."

It was just like Mrs. C to make more work for everybody. She was supposed to have retired last year, when her husband died. If she had, Alvin would still be getting A's and B's, the way he always had, instead of the C+'s she kept giving him this year.

But Mrs. Casey had not retired, even though the school had given her a good-bye party, with presents and a cake—chocolate with white frosting and little pink flowers swirled all over. Whoever picked out that cake had probably never met Mrs. Casey. There was nothing gooey or sweet about her, and she never wore pink, only hard colors, especially dark gray. She looked older than Grandma, but she never got sick or missed a day of school. Nobody in Live Oak could remember having a substitute teacher in Mrs. C's third-grade class.

"Art is a way to tell someone what's inside you," Mrs. Casey said, turning to print another word on the blackboard. "What you feel, how you see things in the world. In that way, art is language, but without words." She finished writing LANGUAGE, then underlined it. "Think of our art exhibit"—she tapped EXHIBIT with the point of her chalk—"as a test of your imagination."

Alvin let out a long, quiet breath. He should have known it was too good to be true. Even when Mrs. C called off a test, there was still a test.

And worse, he might have done all right on this week's Every Monday Spelling Quiz. He had studied for that. But he was going to flunk this art test for sure. He couldn't remember the last time he drew anything. That was little kids' stuff.

Worst of all, in his whole life—he was 8 1/2—Alvin couldn't remember drawing anything that had ever turned out looking like what it was supposed to be.

He stood the brown marker on its fat tip, glanced out the windows at high clouds. If he started coughing at home this afternoon, would anybody notice he was coming down with a cold? Mom and Dad might not even be there, and Grandma would probably be too busy.

Gramps would notice. He would get out the thermometer and start hunting for the cold medicine in the bathroom cabinets. And all the while, Gramps would be thinking up one of those silly notes he loved to write:

> *Alvin was absent yesterday because of a sore throat. We bought him a new one at Sears and now he's fine.*

After Alvin explained how embarrassing those silly excuses were to a third grader, Gramps started writing regular notes, but only after he pretended to write a silly one first and made Alvin listen to it.

With a cough good enough to earn a regular note from Gramps, nobody—not Mom or Grandma or Dad, not even Mrs. Casey—would be surprised when Alvin felt so sick he had to stay home and miss the art exhibit Friday.

2

"Y̶ou OK?" Jimmy Chen had a mouthful of egg salad sandwich. "Sound like you're dying."

Alvin sucked juice through a straw and pretended this had stopped his coughing. "My throat feels a little scratchy. Hurry up and finish so we can start the game."

Jimmy Chen took another big bite of his sandwich. He ate two of them every day, plus potato chips, but he was still as thin as the day he showed up two years ago. He put an elbow on his drawing to keep the wind from blowing it off the table. On his first try for the art exhibit, he had drawn a skyscraper next to a barn. His black lines were so straight, and he hadn't even used a ruler.

"Maybe I should put more windows in the tower," Jimmy Chen said. "The one we lived in was all glass."

There was no way to mistake him for Jimmy Tanner, who didn't look Vietnamese, but since everybody called Jimmy Tanner just "Jimmy," they had to call the new Jimmy something else. Now, a whole year after the original Jimmy had moved away and Jimmy Chen was the only Jimmy in the third grade, everybody still called him "Jimmy Chen," even the teachers.

"That's really good." Cathy was looking over Jimmy Chen's shoulder. She was so short she had to stand on tiptoes to do it. "Where is it supposed to be?"

"In my mind," Jimmy Chen said. "Like Mrs. C said to do."

On a scale of 1 to 10, today's art drill would get a 4, not nearly as bad as some of the ideas about teaching Mrs. Casey had come up with. She called them "exercises." The worst—so far—was the time she made everybody stand up near her old nicked desk and read the lyrics to hit songs as if they were love poems. Talk about embarrassing. Compared to that, today was a breeze.

"Just close your eyes and see what you want to draw," Mrs. C had told the class before lunch. "See every detail, every shadow. Make it so real you can touch it."

It sounded easy enough. Alvin had no trouble seeing the horse he wanted to draw. It was the same one he dreamed about owning: a shiny black stallion with white markings low on its legs. "Spats," Gramps called those patches of white, even though they looked more like socks. Back when he was young and a cowboy and he worked on an actual ranch in Montana, Gramps rode a horse named Spats. It had those same white feet.

Drawing that horse wasn't as easy as seeing it, no matter what Mrs. Casey said. Spats turned out looking more like a glob of brown Jell-O than a horse.

"I'm doing our whole class." Cathy unrolled her drawing. She had taped two pieces of paper together. Her picture was going to take up twice as much space as anybody else's. "Everybody will be in it."

All the faces in her big drawing were smiling. Some of them were so good, they looked real. Alvin could pick out Eddie—the big kid making a muscle in the back row—and Nicole, with her ponytail so long it reached her waist. And Loretta: the cats on her dress gave her away. The boy waving his arms and jumping had to be Brent. That kid couldn't sit still for a second.

Cathy drew mouths that looked like mouths. The

hair in her pictures never looked like a bunch of squiggles coming out of somebody's head. Sometimes the clothes people wore in her drawings had little wrinkles in them at the elbows and knees, just like in real life. Even back when she was in first grade, Cathy was the best artist in school. Last summer she did the mural on the wall outside the principal's office, showing all the grades from kindergarten through junior high and all the different kinds of students who went to Live Oak Valley School.

"This is you, Alvin," Cathy said, pointing to the boy wearing a baseball glove. Pointy head, arms as long as a gorilla, too big feet, Alvin thought. Doesn't look anything like me.

"This me?" Jimmy Chen said.

Cathy shook her head. "That's Roberto. I haven't drawn you yet." She rolled her drawing back up. "This is just a quick sketch, of course. But I think I'll hand it in today."

"Today?" Alvin flattened his folded-up drawing on the lunch table. "I thought we had all week."

"Mrs. Casey needs to OK your picture, silly." Cathy sighed and started walking back toward the third-grade classroom. "Don't you ever listen?"

"Done." Jimmy Chen crumpled his sandwich bag, hiked up his pants, slid his drawing into a back pocket, and ran toward the ball locker. "I'll get the softball."

Alvin couldn't stop watching little Cathy. She probably made up that story about having to turn in a drawing today. He wouldn't have missed hearing Mrs. Casey say that.

He unfolded his picture. Spats hadn't gotten any better since the last time Alvin had looked at him. The only thing that seemed right was the tail. That had a nice flip to it at the end. Anybody could figure out that was a horse's tail.

But there was no hope for the rest of the picture. The head could have belonged on a bird. And the legs were too long and thin, a little like the stilts clowns walked around on in the circus. He couldn't hand this in. Mrs. Casey would give him an *F*.

Worse, she might hold it up for everybody to see: *"Alvin is drawing a horse-bird on stilts, class. Isn't that nice?"*

His hands felt sweaty. From his shirt pocket he pulled the brown marker, uncapped it. He smoothed his drawing on the lunch table and began slashing fat lines across the horse. The tiny bumps and initials carved in the wood of the table made it look as if he were painting little designs everywhere. The outline of his horse started turning into a rough blotch of muddy brown.

Some final quick, tight circles finished the job. Alvin folded the paper—all that brown ink made it feel cool on his hand—jammed the drawing into a back pocket, and ran to join Jimmy Chen and the rest of the guys on the baseball field.

3

The stack of drawings on her desk looked like a heap of old ranch wood. Mrs. C went through the pile, holding up each picture and saying something nice about it.

She wouldn't be able to do that when she came to the crossed-out horse Alvin had turned in yesterday. When she got to his picture, she would hold it up as an example to the whole class of what not to do.

He tried to think of excuses—"The marker kept slipping in my hand"—but who was he kidding? Mrs. C wouldn't buy any excuse. She never did. She even made Roberto do his homework when he was in the hospital having his tonsils out.

Only a few drawings were left in the stack. Alvin raised his hand to ask if he could go to the boys' room. An emergency, he was ready to tell the old teacher.

Mrs. Casey looked right at him, but pretended she didn't see his hand up in the air.

"We'll start our drawing time now," Mrs. Casey said, giving the last picture—red cats and more red cats—to Loretta. "Today, find one part of the drawing you did yesterday and try to make it better."

A miracle. She had forgotten about his picture. Or lost it. That happened with old people. Gramps forgot about lots of stuff—"He doesn't even know who he is half the time anymore," Mom told Dad just last week—and sometimes Grandma couldn't remember where she left her glasses, even when they were on top of her head. Alvin smiled and smoothed a fresh piece of drawing paper on his desk, got out his brown marker.

All of a sudden, Mrs. C was standing next to him. He stopped smiling. "I'd like you to use this today," she said, and handed him a pencil. It was green with a gold O on it. "The lead is very soft. You won't have to press down hard at all."

She was bending close to his face, talking in a whisper now. But every head in the classroom was turned and looking at her: everybody could hear every word she was saying. "I had trouble the first time I tried to draw too."

She didn't give him that sad smile Mom did when she felt sorry for him, like when he came home with a skinned knee or a rip in his favorite baseball jacket. Mrs. Casey just stared at him, her gray eyes bright behind those thick glasses, then she turned and walked back to her desk.

Alvin squeezed the pencil. Most of the kids were still looking at him. He closed his eyes. Instant relief: all those stares disappeared. Then he saw Spats. On the range. By tall mountains capped with snow. He started the pencil moving.

It glided over the paper. It made him smile. This wasn't drawing at all. This was fun.

He could see every detail of Spats now, even those rippling muscles in the legs. His fingers tingled. He could feel the special pencil making a really good horse. So good he had to open his eyes.

Awful.

The head looked like a brown-paper lunch bag. The body had lumps in it. The legs were so thick they looked like they belonged on an elephant. An elephant in knee socks.

He glanced at Mrs. C. She had her little glasses on, the square ones she used to read with. The book in her hands had an orange fish on the cover. He wanted to give her back the pencil and tell her that he hadn't used it. He didn't want her to think her special pencil could have made something as ugly as this drawing of Spats.

Maybe there was a way to fix it. After all, the mane was perfect this time, like real horse's hair hanging long over the neck.

Alvin put the pencil to his lips. He turned his head to see if this lumpy animal looked any better from a new angle. Then he spotted Eddie on the desk behind him, raised up on a knee in his chair and straining to see what that special pencil had made. The big boy was staring so hard his eyes looked crossed, just like last week when he took a swing at a sixth grader who had made fun of Eddie's crew cut and called him Flat Top.

Alvin folded his arms over the paper, lowered his head, and pretended to be deep in thought. He peeked through his fingers at his drawing. There was no saving this one either. It would never look like a horse.

He glanced at Mrs. Casey. Something she was reading in that fish book was making her smile. "Sorry," he heard himself whisper. By the end of the week,

when the art exhibit rolled around, Mrs. C would probably think of Alvin as the worst student she had ever had in all her years of teaching.

He started the special pencil moving, pushing and pulling it in zigzags over this Spats. The soft point made the crossing out easy and fast—so fast that no matter how high big Eddie was stretching in his chair or how hard he was squinting, he didn't have time to figure out what Alvin was up to.

4

He was running between girls playing kickball, waving a paper airplane in his hand and making a sour buzzing like the drone of a big engine. Brent was making a nuisance of himself. Again. At least he didn't like to play baseball. There would be no telling how silly the games would get with that hyper kid racing all over the diamond whenever he felt like it.

On the pitcher's mound, Alvin readied a fastball to Roy, who stepped out of the batter's box to run a hand through his mop of red hair. Suddenly Brent was in right field, practicing his landings. Eddie, playing first base as usual, turned to the outfield: "Get in foul territory! And stop making that stupid sound!"

The human airplane zoomed into the infield. "Airmail. Airmail."

Eddie collared him with a forearm around the neck. "You may be my cousin, but you're still a pain."

"Airmail." Brent struggled to get free, sucking in air and dropping the paper airplane. "Open it up."

The wind kicked the folded white sheet a little way across the diamond toward shortstop, where Jimmy Chen picked it up and shook it open. Alvin stared at the big blob of black in the center of the paper. It looked familiar. Too familiar.

"Hey, that's mine." Alvin stepped off the mound and hurried toward Jimmy Chen, who was trying to make sense of all the lines in the crossed-out drawing.

"You forgot to turn it in," Brent said in a singsong voice. He was skipping up and down the first-base line now, pulling the pockets of his plaid pants inside out. "Found it in your desk."

Eddie grabbed the drawing. Now there would be no way to get it back. And Roy was running out to have a look. And Roberto was racing in from center field. In a second, every boy in class would be passing the picture around, laughing at it. At Alvin.

Brent sped across the infield, sidestepped Roy and snatched the drawing out of Eddie's hands, then ran out toward right field. "If you want to see it," he said, stopping at the edge of the outfield grass, "you have to let me have a turn at bat."

Alvin threw down his glove and ran straight at

Brent. The light-haired boy lost his grin. His thin face got longer all of a sudden. He looked like a scared weasel. He turned to run just as Alvin lowered a shoulder and caught him above the knees—a perfect football tackle.

The crash drove all the air out of Brent in a squeal. He was mostly bones, no muscle, but he never stopped moving his arms and legs. Maybe this was a mistake. Losing a fight to a weakling like Brent would be something no one could live down.

Alvin pinned the skinny boy on his back, climbed on top of him, clamping his knees on Brent's shoulders, just the way Gramps's favorite wrestler, Wild Wrangler West, always did on TV right before he delivered his famous forearm shiver to the throat that sent his opponent out of the ring on a stretcher. As he picked his drawing off the grass, Alvin thought about sending a forearm into Brent's face. He decided not to, but he cocked the punch anyway, just to make the trouble-maker sweat.

Hard fingers sank into his shoulder and jerked him to his feet. He looked up, expecting to see Eddie, who liked breaking up fights almost as much as he liked starting them. Instead, Alvin saw silver hair and

glasses. Mrs. Casey had him. And she was so strong he couldn't get free.

She had Brent too, holding him by his shirt collar. It was the first time the puny kid had stood still all year.

"What is the meaning of this?" Mrs. Casey didn't wait for an answer. "You will both go straight to your desks and sit there—without a sound—until recess is over."

She let go. Alvin's shoulder hurt. It wasn't possible that anybody this old could be that strong. But she was. He glared at Brent, then took a step toward the classroom.

"What's it supposed to be?" Eddie was holding the crossed-out drawing.

Alvin reached out for the paper. It must have slipped out of his hand when Mrs. C pulled him off Brent. "It's a horse," he said. "Give it back."

"That's no horse," Eddie told him. "It's just a bunch of zaggity lines."

"Edward," Mrs. C said, and she didn't have to say anything else. Eddie lowered his head and handed her the drawing. He looked hurt, as if being called by his full name was the worst thing anybody could do to him.

Mrs. Casey studied the picture for a moment, then looked at Alvin.

"I crossed it out," Alvin said, "because it wasn't good enough to turn in. I can't draw."

"Never tell yourself what you can't do," Mrs. Casey said. "If my students learn anything, it's that they shouldn't be the ones who set limits on themselves." Bony fingers folded the drawing back up. The gold wedding band she still wore looked so loose it might slip off. "Some famous artists draw the same thing over and over before they're satisfied with it. I'll bring in some watercolors for you to try tomorrow. Maybe that will help you create something you like." She smoothed his shirt across his shoulders, then handed the drawing back to him. "Now shake hands with Brent."

The weasel-faced kid was grinning, but a dirt clod was stuck to the back of his sandy-colored hair. Seeing that made Alvin smile. He shook Brent's hand, but fast, to prove he really didn't mean it.

"Now you may both go back to the classroom," Mrs. C said. "And walk, please. No running."

The girls had stopped playing kickball and hop-scotch. They were watching. Being forced to walk across the playground with Brent was the worst punishment. Alvin slowed down to let the hyper kid get ahead of him.

"I'll bring in my watercolors for you," Brent said in that singsong voice. "Teacher's pet, teacher's pet." And he darted out of reach, scattering the girls on the hopscotch courts.

Chasing him would only bring more trouble. The folded-up drawing felt warm. Alvin crumpled it into a wad, then tossed it in the air and caught it like a baseball, pretending he didn't really care about it as he passed Loretta, Nicole, and the rest of the girls. But when he got near the classroom, he ripped up the ruined picture and scattered the pieces in the giant garbage bin at the edge of the parking lot.

Even with the lid shut, the blue metal box smelled of rotten bananas and old lunches. It would be a good place to dump Brent. No, that wouldn't work. Brent would probably have the time of his life in there.

5

She set a long wooden box down in front of him and put two little cups at the edge of his desk. "You'll need to fill both of these," Mrs. Casey said, nodding at the water fountain in the back of the room. "I'll go over how to use them after I get the rest of the class started."

Hadn't her special pencil singled him out enough yesterday? Little Cathy had stuck her drawing of the whole class up on the wall already. If he kept getting all this special attention from Mrs. C, maybe Cathy would decide to erase him from that picture, leaving only—the rest of the class.

Mrs. C stood by the blackboard, her mouth moving fast. But all Alvin could hear was that song Dad whistled when he worked on the car—a tune from way back in his high school days that sometimes made

Mom smile and always made Gramps shake his head.

The rest of the class wasn't smiling and they weren't shaking their heads at Alvin. They weren't even staring at him today. Still, it felt as though he was doing something wrong. All he was doing was sitting there. And he hadn't even touched the wooden box yet.

He opened the box. All those colors in the tray—little ovals of red, blue, orange, and more—made him wonder why no one had ever painted a picture of a watercolor set. It was beautiful.

And the brush. Long and thin, the bristles came to a fine point. And so soft. Nothing like the brushes he used to paint model cars and boats. Those were flat and stiff, not really brushes anymore, more like tiny fans, all spread out and hard.

Mrs. Casey's watercolor set was meant for real artists.

Alvin felt a shiver on his neck. He wouldn't be able to blame these watercolors or this brush if he couldn't paint a decent picture of Spats.

He hurried to fill the little plastic cups so he would be ready when Mrs. C was done with the rest of the class. All of them were too busy listening to her—and too afraid of her—to turn around and watch him at the water fountain.

But she saw. She smiled at Alvin—so fast it looked as though she thought it was a mistake in the first place—then she held up two of Eddie's pictures. Trees. A forest of them.

The drawing with one big tree in the center wasn't as good as the one with three big trees in the forest, Mrs. C said, because the picture with three big trees was more balanced. A few more big trees scattered here and there would be even better.

Big Eddie was grinning now and sitting up straighter than usual, as if he couldn't wait to start scattering more big trees on a new drawing today, making the most balanced forest anyone had ever seen.

If Eddie could do it, so can I, Alvin thought. A cup of water in each hand, he took little steps back to his desk. He didn't spill a drop.

She told him how to hold the brush: "Lightly. Never squeeze it."

She told him to paint in the background first—the mountains ("If you see any when you close your eyes"), prairie grasses, wildflowers, trees, clouds, the color of the sky: "Wait for the paint to dry. Take your time. Then paint your horse."

And don't use too much water. Or too little.

And don't put a dirty brush in any oval of color: "Always clean the brush first." One of those little cups of water was for cleaning, the other was for getting the brush wet enough to pick up color to paint with.

Mrs. Casey was taking all the fun out of it. Typical. All those rules. The brush felt heavy. If he messed up with the watercolors, she'd probably get mad at him and tell him she didn't know how anybody could paint that bad, especially after she told him exactly how to do everything. And what could he say to that?

He closed his eyes. He didn't see any mountains or prairie grasses or the horse Gramps called Spats. He saw Mrs. C talking to Mom and Dad at the art exhibit Friday night: *"Your son has flunked watercolors. And markers. Even crayons. There may be something wrong with how the nerves in his arms and fingers connect to his brain."*

But the colors flowed onto the paper just the way Mrs. C said they would. He made mountains. They looked almost real, all brown and rough. He made the grasses look right too—light yellow and stringy, the way they got every summer in the fields where nobody walked.

Even the drips of blue off the brush—too much water—didn't ruin the sky. The brush blended those spatters with ease.

He blew on the page to speed up the drying. Then he started Spats. In black. The hind legs first. Not bad this time. Solid and thick.

Then the tail (it wound up looking like a beat-up broom) and the back (too long?) and the neck (much too short this time for sure), and suddenly the whole painting started to look dark. And strange.

The brush wasn't moving so easily anymore. Every stroke felt shaky, every line looked squiggly. No matter how careful he tried to be, the horse started to look like a squashed giraffe.

A fat, squashed giraffe.

His elbow bumped the edge of his desk. Tiny drops of black splattered the drawing. He bit a smile. "Watercolors are tricky to work with," Mrs. C had warned him. More flicks of the brush. More of those good brown mountains got speckled.

In no time, the blue sky and the tall yellow grasses looked like they had been caught in a long, dirty rain.

He used too much water.

He put a dirty brush in a clean oval of paint.

He spilled some water from the cleaning cup on the painting.

He pressed the brush down hard, flattening it out as he dragged it across the paper.

The colors ran together. It wasn't possible to tell where the mountains started and the grass stopped. The painting didn't look like anything anymore.

He loaded the brush with black paint, ready to turn what was left of Spats into a complete blur.

But Brent snatched the paper and ran to the front of the class. "Hey, look. It's Alvin's famous no-horse."

They all saw. They all laughed. Cathy almost fell out of her chair, she was laughing so hard. Alvin pushed out of his seat, took a step toward Brent. But Mrs. C got there first. She held the hyper kid by the arm and looked ready—and angry enough—to lift him straight up off the floor and shake him until he fell apart.

Then she saw the drawing in Brent's hand. She saw the dirty watercolors in the tray on Alvin's desk. She saw the spilled water, the flattened brush, the paint-spattered wooden box.

Her face went soft. It got quiet in the classroom. Mrs. C looked ready to cry.

She guided Brent back to his chair, sat him down gently. She handed the drawing to Alvin, but didn't look at him. She picked up her brush, dipped it in one of the cups of water, pulled and twisted the bristles with her long fingers until the tip went back to normal. Then she picked up her watercolors and walked back to her desk.

She sat there, cleaning her paint set with a tissue she got from a bottom desk drawer, the one that creaked. She didn't look at anybody until the lunch bell rang.

Then she looked only at Alvin. Those cold gray eyes told him she was going to have him for lunch.

6

He thought about telling her she looked nice in that dark gray dress. Was it new? Maybe that would take her mind off being angry at him.

Mrs. Casey reached into her middle desk drawer, where she kept her little blue book. Everybody said that if your name went into that book, teachers in every grade all the way through high school would hear about it and treat you like a troublemaker.

The book was lying in the corner of the drawer. Long bumpy fingers reached for the blue cover. Alvin shut his eyes.

"I want you to see this," Mrs. Casey said.

He opened his eyes. She was holding a small photograph. A horse: gray-white, with black dots on it.

"An Appaloosa," Mrs. Casey said. "I called him Stormy because he looked like a rain cloud." She put the picture down in front of him. "Horses are so hard to draw. I used this photograph to paint a picture of Stormy. It still hangs in my bedroom." She looked at the horse. "The photo is better."

He sat back, waiting for the scolding to begin, for her to tell him how he had ruined her best set of watercolors.

"Stormy was such a small colt, nobody wanted him. I used to ride him at my friend's ranch." Mrs. C picked up the photo. "Because he was undersized, they were going to sell him." Her eyes got small and hot behind her glasses. "I didn't want him to become dog food."

For the first time in his life, Alvin was glad he didn't own a dog. She must have seen that in his face because she nodded and said, "That's what they did with horses in those days. That or the glue factory."

Turn a horse into glue? How could that be done? And why would anyone want to do it in the first place? This was starting to feel like listening to Gramps talk about his days on the range in Montana, herding cattle on Spats.

She ran a bony finger along the edge of the photo. "I was only in high school, with no job or money. My friend's father gave me two months to raise $100 to buy Stormy. Appaloosas were expensive—even back

then. I washed cars, did a lot of baby-sitting, cleaned out horse stalls. And every day I rode him, I told him he would be my horse."

She had the same sparkle in her eyes now that Gramps got when he talked about his days as a cowboy. She looked happy, as if she were seeing herself as a girl again, riding that small spotted colt. Then she blinked. The gray in her eyes got cold.

"I couldn't raise all the money," she said. "I even thought of stealing him."

No matter how hard he squinted, Alvin couldn't picture Mrs. C as a horse thief.

"My friend's father was so impressed with how hard I worked," she said, "he let me have Stormy for whatever money I had earned—$30, I think. And he threw in a keen English saddle."

"Keen?" Alvin said.

"*Gnarly* to you. Or is it *excellent* now—or *boss*?"

Hearing her use his words made him smile.

She pulled the picture back, studied it. "I've worked hard ever since then. You never get anywhere by quitting. Or by not trying. Owning Stormy taught me that."

"Do you still like horses?"

Her stare looked far away, but she must have heard

him because she sighed: "I once thought of becoming a veterinarian."

"Gramps was a cowboy," Alvin said. "He wishes he still was."

"I learned how rugged—and lonely—the cowboy life was from paintings." Mrs. Casey reached into her middle desk drawer and came out with another photograph. It was a picture of a painting: a horse and a cowboy, surprised by a rattlesnake. There was real fear in the horse's eyes. Its nostrils were wide open, every muscle rippled.

"Frederic Remington," she said. "He was born in the East, yet his paintings and sculptures are like histories of the Old West—full of special knowledge."

Alvin couldn't stop staring at the painting. It looked alive.

"When you get home today," Mrs. C said, "ask your parents—or your grandfather—to take you to the library. You'll find several good books on Remington. Study them." She tapped the painting. "Looking at anything—really seeing it—is the first step in art."

But art was just talent, wasn't it? Having the knack, Gramps would say. You could draw—like Cathy—or you couldn't. Still, looking at the horses this man Remington painted would be easy homework.

"Sounds . . . keen," Alvin said.

Her laugh came so quick it surprised him. It sounded like a roar stuck deep in her throat, and it made her white bangs bounce. She patted his hand. Her fingers felt warm. Just as suddenly, her smile went away and she squeezed his hand. "You must promise me you won't cross out any more of your drawings." She squeezed harder. "Trying—even when it's uncomfortable, even when the task seems impossible—just trying is what brings the greatest rewards. And if you always try your best, sometimes you'll amaze yourself with what you can do."

She let go of his hand. "We're going to hang up your next picture, no matter what it looks like or how much you cross it out."

He couldn't speak. For a moment, he wanted to squeeze her hand back so hard it would make her bumpy fingers hurt.

She was smiling now. "I'm sure your horse will be so good, your mother will want to put it on her refrigerator." Mrs. Casey put the photo of Stormy back in her middle desk drawer. "You may take the Remington picture home. Please bring it back tomorrow."

"Why didn't you become a vet?" he said.

She closed the middle drawer slowly. "Children are more interesting."

"Do you have any? Of your own, I mean?"

Mrs. C stared at her black shoes, then looked straight at him. "Hundreds," she said.

She took a brown lunch bag from the bottom desk drawer and walked through the open doorway. A few seconds later, he could see her through the classroom windows, walking to an empty lunch table on the eighth graders' side of the schoolyard. Before she could unwrap her sandwich or put the straw into her juice box, two junior high girls sat down next to her. They looked happy to see her.

Then three more eighth graders brought their lunches over to her table. They must have told her a joke, because Mrs. C was laughing again, those white bangs bouncing on her forehead.

Maybe it was hearing that story about Stormy, or seeing the picture of her Appaloosa colt—maybe Alvin's eyes weren't working right—but in the bright sunlight, Mrs. Casey didn't look like the old teacher of these teenagers anymore. She looked like one of them.

7

"Don't slam the door." Mom slipped a big brass ring of jangling keys over her wrist and strode through the kitchen to her bedroom. "Gramps might still be napping."

He was. On the couch in front of the TV in the family room. He had the longest eyelashes, just like Alvin, and they looked even longer with his eyes shut. His hands bunched together under his chin in a snarl of fingers—he had broken most of them when he was young and the bones hadn't set exactly right—and his gold wedding band seemed to be holding that crooked ring finger together.

His rerun channel was on. "Hopalong Cassidy" was just ending. Alvin set the heavy library books down on the low table. The one on Frederic Remington was so thick he had worried that the librarian would count it as two books and charge twice as much in fines if he brought it back late. He reached out to nudge Gramps awake and show him the books.

The old man smelled of oranges. He had been out in the grove at the end of the road again, where he wasn't supposed to be because it was private property and the sun was too hot and he always forgot to wear a hat. He had stuffed orange peels in his shirt pocket.

"I left dinner instructions on the kitchen table," Mom said in a whisper from the doorway to the TV room. "Make sure Gramps has his glasses on when he cooks, or you might have spaghetti with taco sauce again."

It didn't taste that bad. Alvin followed her to the kitchen. "We could wait for Grandma to get home."

"You know how her students like to talk after class." Mom had already changed her shoes and put on her new tan blazer, but she hadn't taken off her sunglasses. "Sometimes I think they spend more time talking than they do rug hooking."

One of Grandma's best hooked rugs sat on the floor in the dining room. Roses, all in soft colors. It looked too pretty to be put on the floor. "She's really a good hooker, isn't she," Alvin said.

Mom laughed. "Rug hooker, dear." She hunted through her purse. "That's why the college asked her to teach. It's becoming a lost art."

"So, that kind of talent runs in our family?"

She stared at the roses on the rug. "I certainly didn't get any."

He wanted to tell her, "Me neither, and my teacher's making sure everybody will know that Friday night." But he kept quiet. Mom might not understand, like last summer, when he still had a cast on his wrist and she wouldn't let him play in the last Little League game of the season. He had chipped one of the bones in his wrist riding his bike down by the dry creek bed: tires slick with dew skidded on gravel, throwing him against the smooth boulders lining the bank. Dad said that cast had to come off before he could play baseball. Grandma didn't see how one game, even a league championship game, could be more important than Alvin's health.

But Gramps understood. "If his team wins," Gramps had told Mom and Dad, "he'll feel like he wasn't part of that championship. And if they lose, he'll feel like he let his teammates down by not being there to help them."

That same morning Gramps called the doctor, who

said that as long as Alvin could hold a bat and catch a ball without feeling any pain, he could play. Sitting all alone on the windowsill by his door, the league championship trophy was the first thing everybody saw when they walked into Alvin's room.

He grinned. Gramps would understand about Mrs. Casey. Gramps would think of something to take care of this problem too.

Mom found her check book. Her purse clicked shut. "Dad will be calling to check on you before he leaves work to go to his accounting course." She marched to the study—it was really the office she shared with Dad—and picked up her dark leather briefcase. "My property owners' board meeting should be over by 7:30. Maybe we can watch a video together before you go to bed."

He had seen all the videos they owned at least three times, but he didn't want to hurt her feelings, so he said, "OK."

She kissed the top of his head, then hurried up the hall to the front door and made sure it was locked and deadbolted. "If anything goes wrong, Dad's phone number is—"

"On the message board," Alvin said. "I know what to do, Mom."

She stopped, ran a hand over his hair. "It's just that Gramps is—"

"Old? Ancient? Frail?" Gramps was standing in the doorway of the family room. "Dottie, I'm not help-less—yet."

"Oh, Dad, stop it." Mom kissed him. His hair was sticking out like clumps of silver straw around his ears. "I have to run. Dinner instructions—"

"We'll do fine." Thick crooked fingers waved her away. "Where'd you get those books, Alvy?"

"He made me stop at the library on the way home," Mom said, glancing at her watch. "I'm late."

"So go," said Gramps.

" 'Bye, Mom." Alvin watched her disappear past the refrigerator, where his drawing would go if Mrs. Casey was right. The back door banged shut, the dead-bolt snapped into place. Those twin sounds always made him a little sad: in this house, they meant good-bye. Still, he felt relieved. Everything was always rushed with Mom. He couldn't keep up with her. At the library, she said she couldn't stop to look at the pictures in the Remington book. On her schedule, there wasn't time to do anything except check out the books and drive home. Fast.

Gramps had the Remington book open to a picture of a statue: a cowboy on a bucking bronco. "Now here's a real artist. Look at all the movement in that."

Alvin snuggled close to him. "My teacher said I should study these. To help me draw."

"I thought you were in third grade. What are you doing still drawing?"

"It's a special project."

Gramps paged through the book at the same time he fingered the remote control to turn up the volume on the TV. The Lone Ranger was riding again. In black and white. Almost nothing on this station came in color.

"Are cowboys lonely?" Alvin said.

"Nonsense. Who told you that?"

"My teacher."

Gramps shook his head. "What do these young schoolteachers know about it?"

"Mrs. Casey is old," Alvin told him. "Older than you, I think."

"Ruth Casey?"

"She's making us draw a picture for our art exhibit on Friday night."

"Ruth Casey used to run that school, you know."

Gramps leaned back in the couch and smiled. "She had strawberry blond hair. Wore it in a ponytail all the time." He coughed a laugh. "She's a good ten years younger than me. Probably still pretty, am I right?"

Mrs. C pretty? Alvin blinked. "I can't get anything I draw to look like anything."

"She was a real piece of work," Gramps said. "Nobody on the board of education could ever slip anything past her."

Maybe there was no reason to worry. Everybody in this house would have things to do Friday night. Everyone would be off someplace. Except Gramps. But if nobody reminded him about the art exhibit, Gramps would probably nap right through it. Alvin smiled. "She's still the toughest teacher in the school. Maybe in the whole state."

Gramps squinted at him. "Lucky you."

Lucky? No way.

"She's always telling us what we do wrong," Alvin said. "And how much we don't know."

"Glad somebody is." Gramps flipped a page in the Remington book. He pointed to a man with long blond hair in a painting of Indians on horseback attacking Army soldiers. "Wouldn't want to wind up like General Custer here, would you? Nobody could tell him anything because he thought he was so smart he already knew everything." Rough fingers shut the book hard. "Why do you think you go to school—to find out how smart you are or to learn something?"

The old man pushed up off the couch and started for the kitchen. "If I told you this story already, don't stop me. It's worth hearing again." He cleared his throat. It sounded as though he had a marble stuck in there. "The first time I showed up at Rounders' Camp, Jack Rounders—he owned the Rockin' d Ranch—said I didn't know a thing about cutting steers or riding herd." Gramps winked. "He was right, of course. Took me most of the summer to learn how big a nothing I knew."

This sounded like a new story. "How did you learn?" Alvin said.

"To be a cowboy?" Gramps was squinting at the dinner directions. "I just watched old Jack Rounders. Every move he made. How his wrist snapped just before he threw his rope"—Gramps flicked his wrist in the air—"the way he leaned in the saddle to signal his horse to start and stop in front of a steer"—he jerked from side to side. "Why, I just about studied that cowboy to death. Then I copied what I could and sort of faked the rest." He put a hand on Alvin's shoulder. "Of course, I never let on that's what I was doing. And I wouldn't want anybody else to know about it, either. Your grandma likes the idea that I was a natural-born cowboy."

At the end of the counter, Alvin found the reading glasses—the silver ones that always felt sticky. Gramps put them on and held Mom's handwriting out at arm's length. "So when is it?"

"What?"

"Your art show."

Alvin swallowed air. If he kept quiet, Gramps would probably forget about the whole thing in a minute or two.

"Friday night, did you say?" Gramps put the dinner instructions down and washed his hands at the sink. "Will Ruth Casey be there?"

Alvin swallowed hard. "What if I don't turn in a drawing?"

"You know as well as I do," Gramps said, "she won't let you out of it. Ruth Casey never quit in her life. When she first came out here, nobody'd ever heard of a woman principal. She wasn't about to let that stop her." His smile got fat. Usually, Gramps only smiled like that when he told stories about his days as a cowboy. "No way she'd stand for anybody giving up just because things got a bit tough. No sir, not her style." He squinted at the recipe. "Besides, aren't teachers supposed to get students to do all sorts of things they don't want to do? A little silly, if you ask me, to go blaming her for doing her job."

The only thing on the refrigerator—the only thing likely ever to be put up there—was a coupon for soap, held by a magnet shaped like a mushroom.

"Earth to Alvy." Gramps was smiling over the top of his reading glasses. "You want your macaroni and cheese well done or rare?"

Alvin opened the refrigerator door. "You don't have to go. The art exhibit's really no big deal."

"Wouldn't miss it," Gramps said. "In fact, I'll make sure we all go. Wouldn't hurt anybody in this house to miss a class or a meeting once in a while."

Alvin put the margarine and milk on the counter, then got the box of macaroni and cheese from the bottom shelf of the pantry. Gramps read the instructions on the box and began humming the "Lone Ranger" theme song.

"You shouldn't hide the orange peels in your shirt pocket," Alvin said, turning toward the hall and fighting tears. "Grandma will find them and get mad at you."

He walked to the family room, punched the OFF button on the remote control. The Lone Ranger and Tonto disappeared with a sharp click. If only it could be that easy to make Mrs. C and her art exhibit go away.

No chance, he thought. Paging through the Remington book, every picture began reminding Alvin of how terrible his drawings kept turning out, how awful his Spats was going to look up there next to Eddie's forest and Jimmy Chen's skyscraper. Even Gramps wouldn't be able to recognize his own horse.

Alvin closed the book. He couldn't take any more of those beautiful paintings, and he wasn't sure he could take any more of Mrs. Casey's third grade.

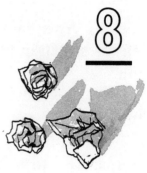

He could tell her the horse was hiding behind one of those little mountains he knew how to draw. "Sure, it's running back there—see this little cloud of dust?" Or that the grass had grown so tall it was covering up the horse. And a horse could lie down and sleep in a gully someplace out of sight, couldn't it?

But Mrs. C wouldn't believe any of it. No point in even asking if he could draw a picture without a horse in it. That would be the same as quitting, and she wouldn't let him do that. She would just point at number 4 on her DOS and DON'TS poster: DO YOUR BEST EVERY DAY.

If he were tall enough to reach that poster, he would rip it up. He stepped into the classroom and walked straight to her desk and handed her the Remington picture she had let him take home last night.

"Did it help?" Mrs. Casey asked.

He shook his head.

She touched a big silver pin on the collar of her blue dress: a horse head inside a thin circle. "I wore this today to bring you luck. Just do your best, Alvin."

Heavy feet took him back to his seat. He stared at the blank piece of drawing paper on his desk.

If he did nothing, if he didn't draw a single line, Mrs. C would still hang it up. "Alvin's Nothing," Brent would probably call that empty piece of paper. "Alvin's Best," Mrs. Casey would tell everybody.

He closed his eyes. No Spats. No mountains. No prairie grasses or sagebrush or flowers. Nothing.

It made him start sweating. The brown marker felt slippery in his hand. Everybody else was drawing something. Rows of arms were moving: Jimmy Chen was drawing his super-straight lines without even using a ruler, Big Eddie was putting in tiny scribbles to make tree bark in his forest, Loretta was making curved tails on every one of her cats.

And my best is nothing.

When he closed his eyes this time, it was to keep the tears inside.

"I just look at the edge of paper and move my hand straight with it." Jimmy Chen drew a line fast and without a wiggle, then another. "You try."

Alvin took the marker. He tried it Jimmy Chen's way. It was the straightest line he had ever made.

"Not bad." Jimmy Chen opened the plastic wrap on his second cheese sandwich. "You can do good buildings like that."

If I was drawing buildings, Alvin thought. Still, he felt good that he had asked his friend for help. If nothing else, he would at least have some nice straight lines on that paper now. That was something.

Maybe Gramps had a good idea when he was young and learning to cowboy: find somebody who really knows how to do a thing, then get him to show you how he does it.

Loretta said she didn't know exactly how she drew ears and eyes—"I never think about it," she told him, "I just draw"—but it looked to Alvin as though she did it with little mounds, made like quick half circles.

He took her red marker and tried it her way. It was easy.

There was nothing easy about the way Cathy drew anything. She had to figure it all out down to the tiniest part. "You wouldn't want a short person like Brent in front to look smaller than a tall person like Jimmy Chen in the back," she told him. "And a wide person like Eddie shouldn't look thinner than a thin person like Joyce just because he's in the last row."

It was a mistake to ask her for help. She knew too much.

"I don't get it." Brent bounced an orange on the lunch table. "Just show him how you'd draw a horse."

Cathy picked up her marker and paper. "I don't teach," she said, and she walked away.

"Look at how I do birds." Brent pulled a blue marker from his back pocket and scribbled on the bumpy skin of the orange: a soft curving line, like a long backward *S*, started the bird, forming the top of the head, the neck, and the round belly. "Easy, huh? You could do birds."

Before Alvin could say anything, Brent ran toward the swings, ripping the orange apart and tossing bits of the peel in the air like confetti.

With a finger, Alvin drew that long backward *S* in the dirt. Even on the dusty ground, it looked more like a horse's neck than anything he had drawn before.

A shadow fell over the *S*. Big Eddie was coming straight at him. Alvin used his shoe to rub out the *S*.

"That little pip-squeak giving you a hard time again?" Eddie helped himself to a piece of apple from Alvin's lunch, then turned to stare at Brent, who was now standing on his head on one of the swings. "I'd slug him, but my mom won't let me."

"He was helping me," Alvin said. "Showing me how he draws birds."

Another piece of cut-up apple disappeared in the big boy's mouth. "How come?"

"I've been asking everybody. So I can see how they make their pictures. So maybe I can draw something that turns out looking like something."

Eddie frowned, put his sneaker on the table, and leaned in close. "How come you didn't ask me?"

The apple Alvin had been chewing tasted sour. He couldn't swallow.

"If I show you how I draw trees," Big Eddie said, "will you come play softball with us? We need you to pitch."

Alvin nodded and watched the thick-chested boy pick up a twig and start drawing in the dirt, right where the rubbed-out backward *S* had been. Eddie drew fast, especially when it came to the tree bark, which was really nothing more than a bunch of quick squiggles here and there.

"There," Eddie said. "That's how I do it. Now, come on." He headed toward the softball field. "We don't have much time left before class."

Those squiggly lines looked easy to make. Alvin picked up the twig and tried it. When those lines weren't inside the outline of a tree, they looked like hair. Maybe even a mane. Or a tail.

"Hey, let's go." Big Eddie had his hands on his hips near the swings, now empty of Brent and full of small first graders. "I haven't had a turn at bat yet."

Alvin took one more look at the lines in the dirt, then dropped the twig and started running to join Eddie.

He kept staring at the picture. It didn't seem possible that he had drawn this.

It wasn't great—nothing that any real artist like

Frederic Remington would get excited about—but anyone could tell this was supposed to be a horse. The ears weren't very good—they weren't sharp pointed enough—and the mouth wasn't right—horses didn't grin, did they?—but all in all, it really looked more like a horse than anything else. A horse standing in short grass in front of mountains.

All he had to do now was color it in.

He decided not to. He put dots on the horse instead. Like the markings of an Appaloosa. He left the feet white, like on the real Spats.

This wasn't Mrs. Casey's Stormy and it wasn't Gramps's old horse. This one felt like it belonged to Alvin.

He put the drawing down on her desk. Mrs. C stopped reading the history textbook and took a long look at the picture.

She pulled the paper closer. She picked it up. She put it down. She smiled at him.

That smile felt good. Especially good. Because he knew he had earned it.

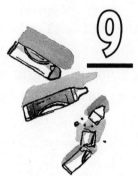

In front of a crowd of parents and kids by the far wall, Cathy was standing on a chair next to her big drawing. It had grown to three full pieces of paper. She used a new pencil to point to the red-haired boy in the picture and said, "This is Roy."

Roy's mother said, "Ooh," and looped her arm around her husband's elbow. Roy grinned. In that picture he had bigger arm muscles than anybody except Eddie.

Alvin walked away. Someone had cleared the center of the room by sliding all the desks against the walls. Alvin found his by the cabinet near the bookcases. Even all the way over here, he could still hear Cathy's voice.

"And this is Roberto," the short girl was saying, pointing to a thin boy with black eyes and a baseball bat on his shoulder.

Roberto's parents smiled at each other.

At the edge of that crowd, Mom shook her head. "Look at all the different styles of dresses she drew."

"Every kid seems to be doing something." Dad had on the tie Mom made Alvin give him for a birthday present this year. It had white swans all over it. He never wore this tie to work. "See that boy she has standing on his head on the swing?"

Grandma was wearing her big glasses. "She does hands very well. Can you find Alvin in there?"

Any second now Gramps would say something about how wonderful this drawing was. But Gramps was still over by the door, talking to Mrs. Casey. In her yellow dress and shoes to match, she looked like somebody's aunt tonight.

"Didn't know you liked horses." Nicole fingered her long brown ponytail. "My uncle has two. He lets me ride them whenever I want." She stared at the big drawing of everybody in class. "I wish my mom had seen my picture before she saw that one." She turned to stare at her drawing, taped on the wall near the cabinet: long-stemmed flowers lying on a picnic table. "Maybe then she would like mine more."

"Me too." Alvin spotted his horse hanging in back, over the water fountain, Jimmy Chen's skyscrapers on one side, Eddie's forest on the other. Mrs. C must have liked all three drawings to put them up there, where everyone would be sure to see them because everyone would go back there for a drink at least once tonight.

"Does it have measles?" Brent cut in front of Jimmy Chen to get to the water fountain first. "I had measles. Spots all over me." He had white glue in his hair, matting it down behind his ear. "Pretty good, though. Better than how my birds turned out."

Alvin pointed to the neck and the back of his horse. "The way you make birds is how I drew this part."

Brent stopped slurping water just long enough to take a closer look. He shrugged, then zoomed back toward the crowd near Cathy's drawing.

"You should have put a building in there." Jimmy Chen folded his arms across his chest. "Maybe a whole town back by that mountain."

"Too tough for me." Alvin pointed to the legs of his horse. "I had enough trouble with these straight lines you showed me how to make."

The thin boy squinted, then blinked. "Told you you could do it. But you still need a barn or something."

A barn—a small one—would look nice.

"Where's your cat?" Loretta leaned over the water

fountain to get close to the horse. "Did you forget how to draw it?"

"I used what you showed me here." He pointed to the horse's eyes and ears.

She rubbed the cat pin on her dress. "Ears should be more pointy on a horse, shouldn't they?"

Horses ears did look a lot like long, sharp leaves. Maybe he could get Nicole to show him how she drew those leaves on her flower stems.

"Looks OK to me." Eddie muscled his way to the water fountain. "Only, where's the trees?"

"There are no trees out on the buffalo range," Loretta told him.

"Sure there are," Eddie said.

"See his mane?" Alvin said. "I drew it the way you do tree bark. The tail too."

The big boy pushed himself up on the water fountain and put his nose to the drawing.

"Edward." Mrs. Casey led Gramps and Grandma and Mom and Dad toward the back. "Get down before you break school property."

"Which one is yours, son?" Dad said.

Alvin pointed to his horse.

"Why, it's lovely." Mom sounded surprised.

"Maybe you got some of Grandma's artistic talent after all."

"Of course he did." Grandma put on her small glasses and moved closer to the drawing. "I should have you make this as a rug design. For your room."

"It's a horse, isn't it?" Dad said.

"Appaloosa," Gramps said. "But what's this?" He touched the white feet on the horse. His mouth opened, but no sound came out. He stepped back, put his hand on Alvin's shoulder, and gave him a long squeeze. "I'd like to frame this and hang it in the family room, Alvy. So I can look at it. Every day."

Better than on the refrigerator. Much better.

"It is a very sturdy horse, Alvin," Mrs. Casey told him. "And I especially like the way he holds his head up."

Alvin looked at his shoes. Mom had made him wear the heavy brown ones tonight. "I've been thinking about ways to make it better. But even then, I don't think I'll ever be able to draw anything really good."

"Really well." Mrs. C bent down and whispered, "I knew they would like it." She smiled. "I'm so proud of you for not giving up."

"Didn't I tell you she wouldn't let you quit?" The

old cowboy laughed, then nodded at Mrs. Casey. "Like I've said for over 20 years now, this school's lucky to have you as a teacher."

Behind those thick glasses, her pale gray eyes looked soft and wet. "It's moments like this—when a student tries so hard he learns to do something he thought he couldn't do—that make me feel like the lucky one."

Alvin couldn't move, couldn't swallow. For an instant, he wanted to hug Mrs. C—but all the people here, especially Brent and Eddie, would never stop laughing if they caught him hugging a teacher.

"What's all the fuss about back here?" Little Cathy pushed her way through the ring of bodies. She looked straight at Alvin's drawing, then at Alvin. Her face got sour.

The best artist in the class, in the whole school, and she was going to hate his picture. And she was going to say so. And everybody would have to agree with her and take back all the nice things they had said. Even Gramps.

If Mom had only let him wear his running shoes, Alvin could race out of here fast now, before Cathy spoiled everything.

"I taught him how to do the legs," Jimmy Chen told Cathy.

"He got the eyes from me," Loretta said.

"The mane and the tail"—Eddie pointed to his forest—"are just like my tree bark. See?"

"Big deal." Now wearing a headband of blue construction paper, Brent jumped up and tapped the back and neck of the horse. "I showed him how to make the important part." He discovered Dad's swans. "Excellent tie."

Cathy didn't look angry anymore. She looked puzzled. She pointed to the tiny curved lines around the horse's eyes. "Who taught you how to do these?"

"The eyelashes?" Alvin said. "No one."

Jimmy Chen patted him on the back. "That's Alvin's own special touch."

Cathy frowned at the drawing, then marched through the crowd, straight to her desk. She picked out a pencil and climbed on the chair next to her big picture.

With quick strokes, she drew eyelashes on Roberto's face. Then she stepped down and studied what she had done. She nodded. "This will make everybody look so much better." She turned and lost her frown. "Thank you, Alvin."

And she climbed back on the chair and began drawing eyelashes on every one of the faces in her picture.

"It seems you're the one who taught us something tonight." Mrs. Casey drew Alvin to her side and gave him a soft, one-armed hug. "All of us."

Alvin's smile felt as big as the mountains.